FRED & ANTHONY

ESCAPE FROM THE NETHERWORLD

By Esile Arevamirp
With Elise Primavera

Hyperion Books for Children/ New York

First Edition
1 3 5 7 9 10 8 6 4 2

Printed in the United States of America
ISBN-13: 978-0-7868-3677-2
ISBN-10: 0-7868-3677-6
Library of Congress Cataloging-in-Publication Data on file.
Reinforced binding
Visit www.hyperionbooksforchildren.com

RAINDROPS KEEP FALLING ON MY HEAD Words by Hal David; Music by Burt Bacharach © 1969
(Renewed 1997) NEW HIDDEN VALLEY MUSIC, CASA DAVID and WB MUSIC CORP. All rights reserved.
Used by permission of ALFRED PUBLISHING CO., INC.
RAINDROPS KEEP FALLING ON MY HEAD From BUTCH CASSIDY AND THE SUNDANCE KID
Lyrics by Hal David; Music by Burt Bacharach © 1969 (Renewed) Casa David, New Hidden Valley Music,
and WB Music Corp. International Copyright Secured. All rights reserved.

Disclaimer:
This book contains excerpts from
The Guide to the Netherworld.
We are not responsible for any loss and/or damage
to personal property or to your personal person.
Should you decide to take any of this seriously,
we strongly recommend bringing a change of
underwear and a toothbrush.

This book is dedicated to Steve Malk,
Pez lover—and the guy who continues
to help me make some dough

FRED

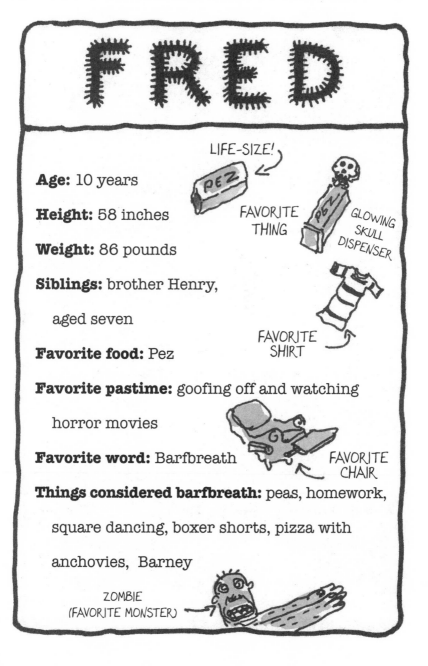

Age: 10 years

Height: 58 inches

Weight: 86 pounds

Siblings: brother Henry,

aged seven

Favorite food: Pez

Favorite pastime: goofing off and watching

horror movies

Favorite word: Barfbreath

Things considered barfbreath: peas, homework,

square dancing, boxer shorts, pizza with

anchovies, Barney

LIFE-SIZE!

FAVORITE THING

GLOWING SKULL DISPENSER

FAVORITE SHIRT

FAVORITE CHAIR

ZOMBIE (FAVORITE MONSTER)

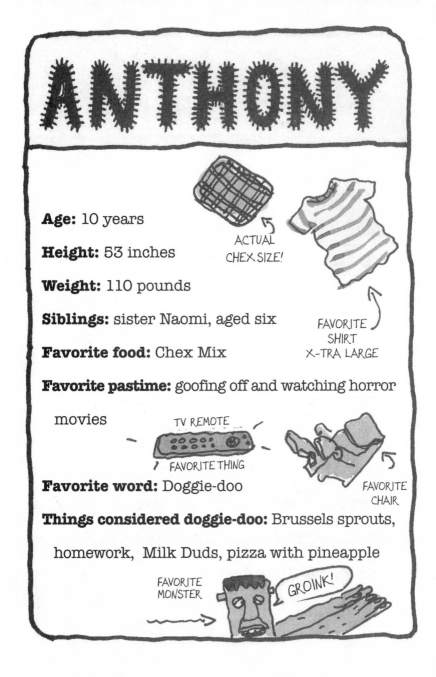

ANTHONY

Age: 10 years

Height: 53 inches

Weight: 110 pounds

Siblings: sister Naomi, aged six

Favorite food: Chex Mix

Favorite pastime: goofing off and watching horror

movies

Favorite word: Doggie-doo

Things considered doggie-doo: Brussels sprouts,

homework, Milk Duds, pizza with pineapple

ACTUAL CHEX SIZE!

FAVORITE SHIRT X-TRA LARGE

TV REMOTE

FAVORITE THING

FAVORITE CHAIR

FAVORITE MONSTER

GROINK!

3

1. FRED

red and Anthony hung out a lot together, goofing off and watching horror movies.

GETTING OUT OF WORK.
Their foolproof way of Getting Out of Work was . . .
PAYING SOMEONE ELSE TO DO IT.

Smaller sisters, younger brothers, or kids like the one who, on a bet, ate a Frito that had been sitting under a seat on the school bus for three weeks, were usually hired.

In Fred and Anthony's never-ending pursuit of Getting Out of Work, Paying Someone Else worked beautifully.

THERE WAS ONLY ONE THING . . .

HOW MUCH?

2

CASH FLOW

Fred and Anthony had none.

It was around six o'clock and almost dark one Saturday night. Fred and Anthony were at The Grand Marquis Alucard's Video Store. (It had a fancy name, but was kind of a dump.)

They were returning *Abbott and Costello Meet Dr. Jekyll and Mr. Hyde*, *Abbott and Costello Meet Frankenstein*, and *Abbott and Costello Meet the Invisible Man*. The boys had decided they would watch every horror movie ever made, and they had started with *A*.

Anthony picked up *Attack of the Killer Tomatoes!*

It was completely dark now. From behind the EMPLOYEES ONLY door came the Grand Marquis himself, looking pasty-faced and less than grand in Bermuda shorts.

11

In Fred's basement, *Attack of the Giant Leeches* was coming on TV.

There was a refrigerator full of stuff to drink.

There was Pez and Chex Mix. There was even one of those round red things, a

what-do-you-call-it?—oh, yeah, that's right, an apple.

Better yet, the movie title started with an *A.*

It was going to be a perfect Saturday night, after all.

THERE WAS ONLY ONE <u>OTHER</u> THING.

THE HORRIBLE, HIDEOUS HISTORY PROJECT

Fred and Anthony had a horrible, hideous history project due on Monday morning. They had to build a replica of the Alamo out of Popsicle sticks.

Fred turned off the TV.

"We might as well just get to work," he said glumly.

"Wash your mouth out with soap," Anthony answered. Anthony knew from having his mouth washed out with soap, too. But Fred was right; they had work to do.

Fred's brother would have made the Alamo for them.

Anthony's little sister would have made the Alamo for them.

The kid who, on a bet, ate a wad of gum that had been stuck to the bottom of his desk for three weeks would have made the Alamo for them. For a price, that is.

Fred and Anthony needed to make some . . .

In the past, their dough-making ventures had not gone well. Their last one, Fred & Anthony Dog Walking, Inc., had ended when Snowball the cocker spaniel got loose and was sick for a week after eating a can of bacon grease.

QUICK DOUGH 3

17

The first thing Fred and Anthony did was to come up with a catchy title for their book that was going to make them richer than the queen of England.

19

I'M GOING TO HAVE A BUTLER BRINGING ME BOWLS OF CHEX MIX.

And no doubt they would have, except for . . .

A BIG BUT

21

Fred's grandmother called down to him. She had mistakenly thrown out her dentures in a napkin and needed Fred to go through the garbage and find them.

Blood and guts were all right, but false teeth?

Anthony cringed, but Fred's eyes lit up, because suddenly he had a new plan for how to make some Quick Dough.

27

Fred and Anthony went to where they knew the old people were. But the old people knew who Fred and Anthony were. There had been enough botched snow-shoveling jobs, soggy-paper deliveries, grass cuttings where the

flowers had been mowed down, and car wash-
ings where the windows had been left open, so
that all the old people knew to bolt their doors
the minute they saw the two boys.

Fred and Anthony rode to the outskirts of town.

This was where none of the old people knew them.

This was where it was deserted. The sky grew cloudy, and there was a roll of thunder and a crack of lightning.

Unfortunately, this was also where the wheel fell off Anthony's skateboard.

Fortunately, there was a house nearby.

31

HOUSE of the GOOEY DEATH

5

The rain started pouring down in buckets.

"If I didn't know better, heh-heh," Fred laughed nervously as he ran up the porch steps, "I'd say the next thing that happens is we get trapped inside a haunted house."

"You don't really believe in that doggie-doo, do you?" Anthony replied.

"You just said doggie-doo-doo," Fred snickered.

Anthony shrugged and rang the doorbell.

The door creaked open, and there was the oldest old person they'd ever seen.

The old lady reached out a clawlike hand, and with surprising strength pulled both boys inside.

The house, meanwhile, was acting exactly the way a haunted house usually acts. The walls started oozing slime. The doors began bulging and pulsating in a rhythmic, haunted house–heartbeaty way.

THUD
THUD

35

36

Fred and Anthony were pushed farther into the bowels of the house. And if you think the word "bowels" is funny, then you are not taking this story very seriously. Seriously, Fred and Anthony were trapped in a haunted house. And to make matters worse, Fred turned around, and Anthony was gone!

HE LOOKS KIND OF FAMILIAR. DON'T YOU THINK, ANTHONY?

ANTHONY??

42

43

44

GUIDE to the NETHERWORLD

AWESOME!

TIP #1

here are many points of entry to the Netherworld right under your nose! You just haven't noticed them because they are cleverly disguised behind OUT OF ORDER signs on public restroom stalls, Porta Potties, boiler rooms, broom closets, as well as guest powder rooms in haunted houses.

WELCOME!

"I am . . . um . . . ah . . . Dr. Nietsneknarf—
that's it," a very short man with a very long
comb-over in a white lab coat said. "And this is
my assistant, Rogi."

Fred and Anthony looked around. They had
landed in a room with a single chair, some
drills, and a sink the size of a Frisbee to spit
into. It looked exactly like a dentist's office—
except for the monster, made up of stapled-
together old, dead body parts, strapped to a

table over in the corner.

The doctor grinned. "Are you all right?? I hope you didn't hurt your HEADS! Because I couldn't stand to think of anything happening to those wonderful BRAINS!"

"Gee, thanks, Doc," said Fred. "We're really fine."

"Yeah," said Anthony.

"Are you sure I can't get you anything for your HEADS?" Dr. Nietsneknarf asked. "Water? Tea? Chex Mix? Pez?"

"No offense or anything," Anthony said, "but, considering that you're down here in the Netherworld and all, shouldn't you be a mad scientist?"

"You boys are perfect!" The doctor rubbed his hands together. "Now, I think you should rest—you had quite a fall on your HEADS. Just step into my waiting room, make yourselves comfortable, and I shall be with you in a moment."

8

FRANTHONYENSTEIN

But Fred and Anthony were one step ahead of Dr. Nietsneknarf!

They remembered the graying archaeologist in *Curdled Mummy Maniacs*, who had become a curdled mummy maniac after drinking the poisoned cappuccino. There was the plucky investigator in *Curse of the Pod People*, who had become a pod person after eating the jelly doughnut with the pod pill in it. And how could they forget the greedy plantation owner in *Mafia Zombie Lunatics*, who had become a zombie lunatic after a meal of baked ziti and meatballs? No, they had seen too many horror movies to fall for the old Chex Mix and Pez trick—that one was as old as the hills!

DUDE, WE GOTTA GET OUT OF HERE.

YO, I KNOW.

57

GUIDE to the
NETHERWORLD
TIP #2
Contrary to popular belief, the folks down in the Netherworld are very playful when it
MAYBE THIS WILL HELP.

comes to words! They jumble, spell things backward, and use puns. So be on your guard!

HA! HA! THIS BOOK IS REALLY LAME!

THEY SPELL THINGS BACKWARD . . . THEN I WOULD BE DERF!

AND I WOULD BE YNOHTNA.

AND DR. NIETSNEKNARF WOULD BE . . .

Fred and Anthony burst into the doctor's office.

"You're not Dr. Nietsneknarf and Rogi!" they yelled. "You're Dr. FRANKENSTEIN and IGOR!"

"The *evil* Dr. Frankenstein the Third, D.D.S., and his loyal body-snatching assistant, Igor!" Dr. Frankenstein chuckled malevolently.

"*Boys.* They are always trying to get out of work and they NEVER floss!" He shook his head. "Truly revolting!"

"I'm sorry, what did you say your names were?" the doctor asked.

"Fred," said Fred.

"Anthony," said Anthony.

"I'll call him—Franthonyenstein!" Dr. Frankenstein laughed maniacally. "And soon I will create an army of boy-brain creatures—the world will no longer be safe from slackers and gingivitis! Ha! Ha! Ha! Ha! Ha!"

UM, DOC? EXCUSE ME?

"Yeah, well, you're no prize package either, Doc," Anthony said.

"SILENCE!!" Dr. Frankenstein demanded. "I am going to reanimate my monster with your boy-brains!

For any of you out there, now would be a good time to go as well—before the exciting blood-and-guts chapter. We'll just wait here while you do. . . .

EXCITING! BLOOD AND GUTS CHAPTER 9

NOW, WHERE WAS I?

YOU WERE GOING TO DESTROY THE WORLD!

ho says watching TV makes kids fat, rots their tender young minds into jelly brains, and reduces their attention spans to a millisecond, making it impossible for them to retain any information? Well . . . at least it doesn't make it impossible for them to retain information, because Fred and Anthony distinctly remembered something from TV. In the horror movie *The Thing That Ate the Planet That Wouldn't Die*, they learned that you cannot destroy the world by creating an army of boy-brain creatures without a Boy-Brain-Extracticator-World-Destroyalator-Machine—and they told the doctor this.

OH, YEAH?

What Fred and Anthony didn't know was that every mad dentist worth his control-grip toothbrush owns one of these babies. Sure enough, in the corner, hiding behind a potted palm, was a shiny new Boy-Brain-Extracticator-World-Destroyalator Machine.

Performing root canals and body snatching must have required a lot of upper body

strength, because Dr. Frankenstein and Igor
turned out to be in pretty good shape. They
scooped up Fred and Anthony with ease, all
set to de-brain them both.

Fred and Anthony were goners for sure, but on the bright side, at least they wouldn't have to make the Alamo out of Popsicle sticks anymore. On the not-so-bright side, Fred would never have a Pez fountain, and Anthony would never have a butler bringing him bowls of Chex Mix—which was really a bummer, because everybody has to have a dream.

The thought of this gave Fred a sudden, overwhelming urge to use his favorite word. This was a good thing, because it gave Dr. Frankenstein a sudden, overwhelming urge to brush his teeth.

He dropped Fred and went screaming to the bathroom.

Next, Fred pulled out his glowing-skull dispenser and flipped the head back, with the idea that he would shoot a Pez straight into Igor's eye.

But you know as well as I do that a Pez dispenser does not shoot, it dispenses, which is exactly what happened. It delivered a delicious candy treat instead.

SLAM!

What happened next was very horrible indeed.

There was a buzz-saw sound and some squishy, squashy noises. Just when Fred and Anthony didn't think they could take any more, out popped a brain the size of a pea.

BUZZ-Z-Z

BUZZ

SQUASH!

SQUISH!

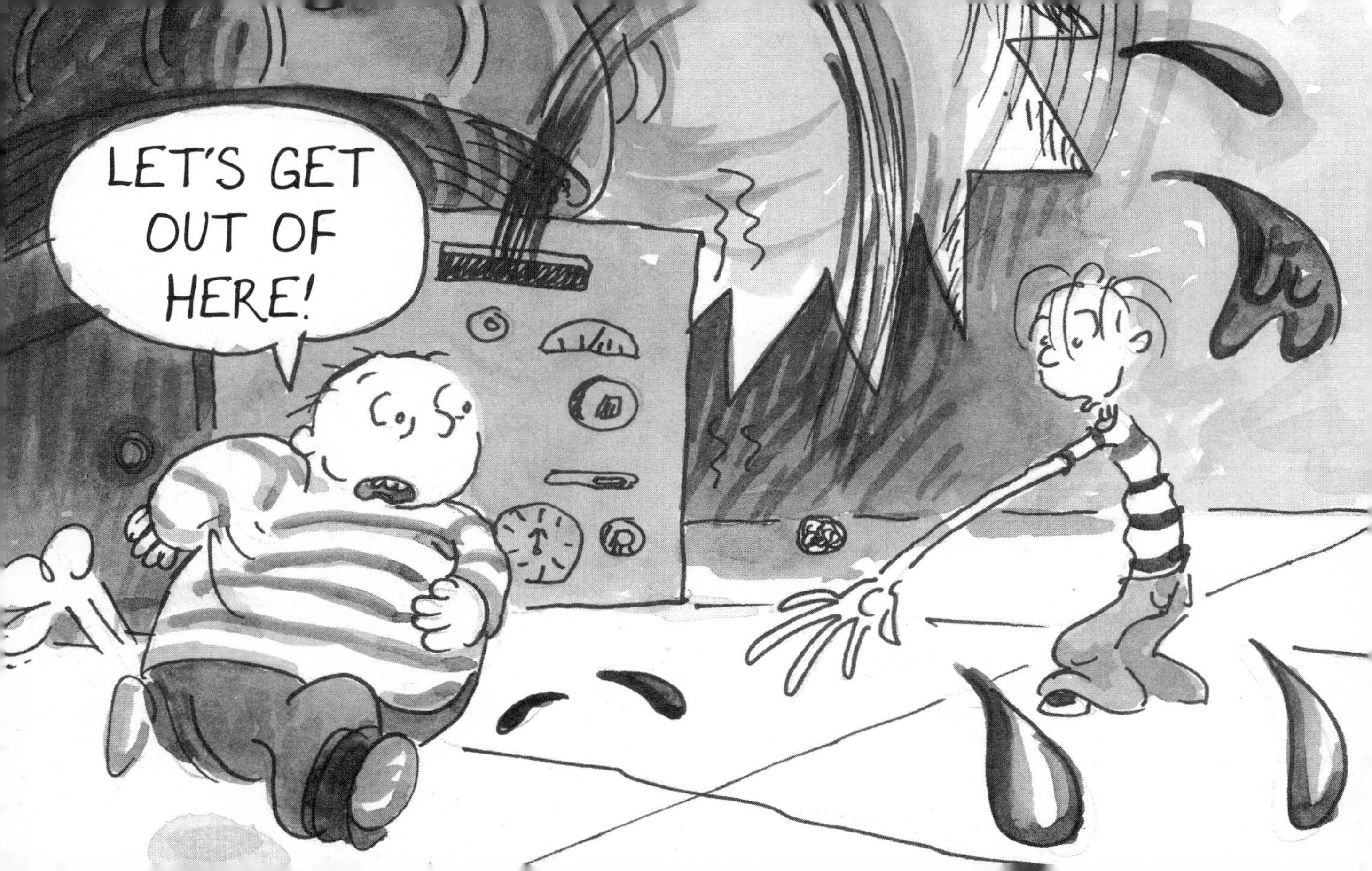
LET'S GET OUT OF HERE!

Unfortunately, Dr. Frankenstein was back,
having freshened his breath and whitened his
teeth by gently cleaning away surface stains.

He grabbed the boys, and they were about to
meet the same horrible fate as Igor, when out
of the shadows stepped a neatly dressed man
in corduroy pants and a work shirt.

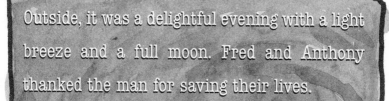

Outside, it was a delightful evening with a light breeze and a full moon. Fred and Anthony thanked the man for saving their lives.

WHAT A NICE GUY.

YEAH, BUT HE REALLY KIND OF NEEDS A SHAVE, BECAUSE HE'S STARTING TO LOOK LIKE . . .

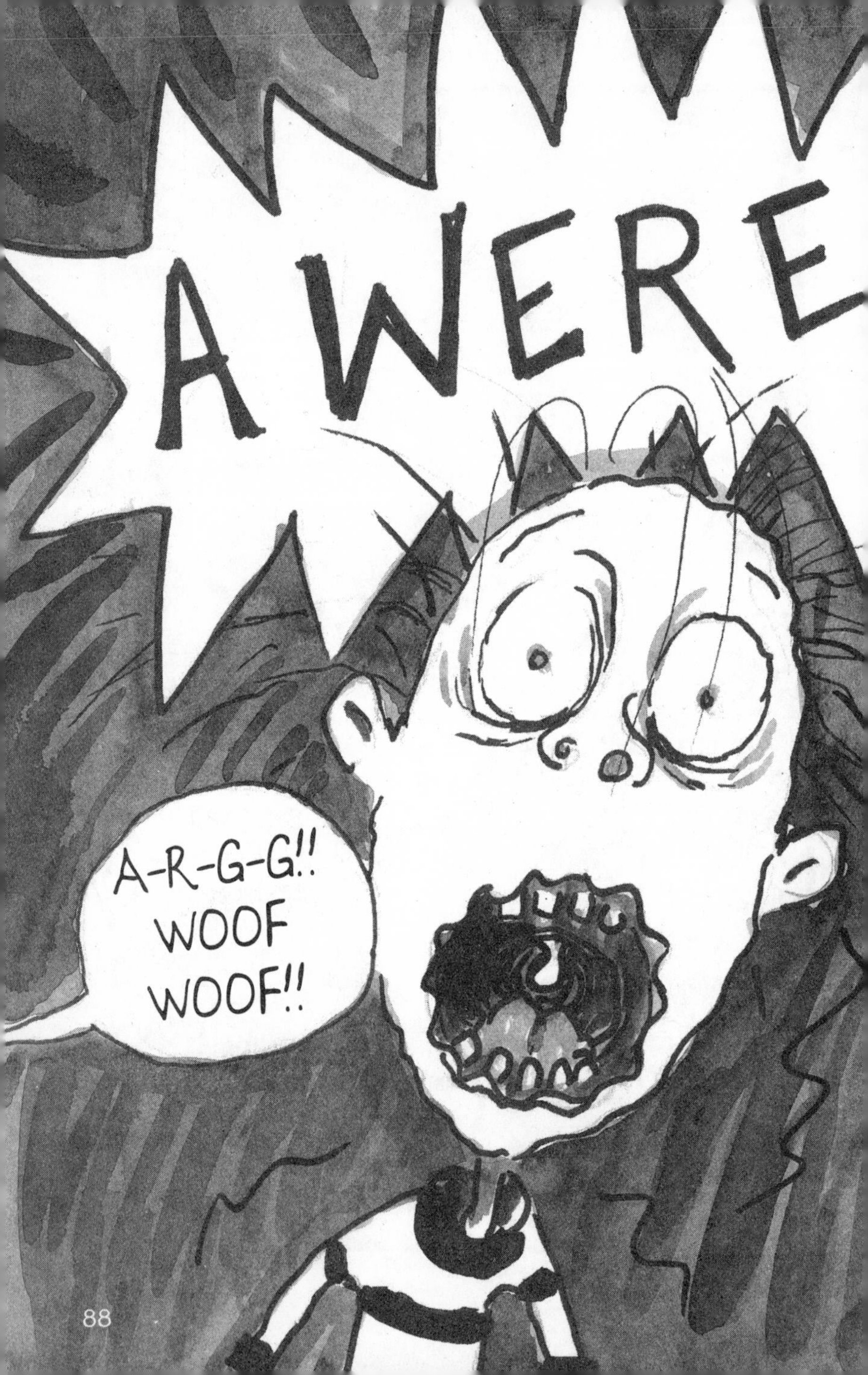
AWERE
A-R-G-G!! WOOF WOOF!!

89

Fred's and Anthony's lives were far from saved. In fact, they had to run, if they were ever going to live to see another horror movie or eat another pack of Pez or bowl of Chex Mix. They ran past houses that looked like giant gravestones and past graveyards with dead trees with blood and guts hanging off them.

Faster and faster they ran, which wasn't
so easy for two kids who sat around all day
in La-Z-Boys. Past ghosts, monsters, hands
crawling out of the graves, they ran, and ran,
and ran, toward a castle that loomed in the
distance.

BLOOD
+
GUTS
←

ZOMBIES
→

Up the drawbridge they raced, and reaching the door at last, they yanked it open.

Gasping for breath, they fell inside, slammed the door shut, and bolted it tightly.

You can only imagine how relieved Fred and Anthony were. They had escaped the Werewolf, Dr. Frankenstein, and all the ghosts, monsters, and blood and guts.

97

The bat changed, as they do, and if you haven't figured out by now that the Grand Marquis Alucard was really Count Dracula, then you should start paying better attention to this story.

WHY DON'T YOU JUST CALL YOURSELF DRACULA, ALREADY?

And if you think the Count was going to turn the boys into vampires, then you are dead wrong. By pure luck, he had a digestive problem with excessive gas and bloating, which had forced him to trade in sucking blood for cherry Popsicles years ago.

LOOK INTO MY EYEZ-Z-Z! TELL ME VAT YOU SEE-E-E-E-E-E!

UM, EXCUSE ME A MINUTE, COUNT. WE NEED SOME NEW MATERIAL FOR A BOOK WE'RE WRITING THAT'S GOING TO MAKE US RICHER THAN THE QUEEN AND ALL; AND THAT WHOLE HYPNOTISM THING HAS BEEN DONE TO DEATH.

COULD YOU NOT USE THAT WORD?

The Count's Popsicle diet was a happy twist of fate for the boys—plus, as you know, they could use the sticks.

Grabbing as many of these as they could, Fred and Anthony decided to leave the Netherworld, go home, and get busy building the Alamo.

BUT YOU KNOW, I COULD USE SOME HELP AROUND THIS PLACE—A LITTLE CLEANING, A LITTLE IRONING . . .

HELP?

AS IN WORK?

Fred and Anthony wound up in a room, which, not surprisingly, turned out to be behind the EMPLOYEES ONLY door in the Grand Marquis video store.

The boys were so relieved and grateful to be alive that they swore they would stop taking advantage of younger brothers and sisters, the kid who would eat anything for money, and old people the world over. Sitting around watching horror movies and eating Pez and Chex Mix all day wasn't such a constructive way to spend their time either, they decided.

We here at the Netherworld hope you have enjoyed your visit—in fact we are just dying for you to come back!
WARNING: Upon leaving the Netherworld, make sure that you are not followed home by any P.P.'s (paranormal phenomena).
DISCLAIMER: The Netherworld holds no responsibility for anything—hence the name "NETHER" as in "NON", meaning no responsibility—GOT IT?
Count Dracula
President and Chief Spokes-phantom
The Netherworld
THANK YOU, DEAR. SUCH A GOOD BOY.
I'M NOT OVER MY WRITER'S BLOCK— ARE YOU?
NO.
BUMMER.

YOU KNOW, FRED, MAYBE WE OUGHT TO ALERT THE AUTHORITIES ABOUT THE PRESENCE OF THIS DANGEROUS SUBTERRANEAN WORLD LURKING BENEATH OUR HUMBLE TOWN.

YOU'RE RIGHT, ANTHONY. ON THE OTHER HAND, WE COULD ALWAYS CHARGE ADMISSION.
GUIDE TO THE NETHERWORLD
I WOULDN'T DO THAT IF I WERE YOU.

Sadly, Fred and Anthony never did get over their writer's block, but their story does have a happy ending, for Fred and Anthony learned some important lessons. They learned about taking responsibility, about doing the right thing, about being all that they can be, about never giving up, about following their dream, about growing up, and about believing in who they are.

But, dear reader, the best part was that they made new friends along the way.

117

And who could blame the poor things if they took a break from their life of good deeds to kick back with some Pez, Chex Mix, and a horror movie from time to time?

Yes, that Fred and Anthony were two special boys!

They still had to build the Alamo. Now,
that's scary.

FRED AND ANTHONY HUNG OUT A LOT TOGETHER, GOOFING OFF AND WATCHING HORROR MOVIES. IN ORDER TO HAVE ALL TH-